VIKING
Published by the Penguin Group
Penguin Putnam Books for Young Readers, 345 Hudson Street, New York, New York 10014, U.S.A.
Penguin Books Ltd, 27 Wrights Lane, London W8 5TZ, England
Penguin Books Australia Ltd, Ringwood, Victoria, Australia
Penguin Books Canada Ltd, 10 Alcorn Avenue, Toronto, Ontario, Canada M4V 3B2
Penguin Books (N.Z.) Ltd, 182-190 Wairau Road, Auckland 10, New Zealand

Penguin Books Ltd, Registered Offices: Harmondsworth, Middlesex, England

First published in 2000 by Viking, a division of Penguin Putnam Books for Young Readers.

5 7 9 10 8 6 4

LIBRARY OF CONGRESS CATALOGING-IN-PUBLICATION DATA
Schnur, Steven.
Spring thaw / by Steven Schnur ; illustrated by Stacey Schuett.
p. cm.
Summary: Describes spring's gradual arrival on a farm.
ISBN 0-670-87961-4 (hc)
[1. Spring Fiction. 2. Farm life Fiction.] I. Schuett, Stacey, ill. II. Title.
PZ7.S3644Sp 2000 [E]—dc21 99-22543 CIP

Manufactured in China
Set in Galliard

For Elizabeth,
my harbinger of spring
STEVEN

For Ian
—STACEY

It begins with a warm wind late at night,
sighing through the hemlock trees,

swaying branches, and shaking loose the heavy snow
that fell all day and turned fields and frozen lakes and
distant rooftops white.

The old house begins to creak as wooden floors breathe in the warm moist air. Water trickles from the roof, drop by drop.

A raccoon stirs in its winter den, then climbs up into the snow, its dark eyes shining in the white light of the rising moon.

A round-bellied doe pauses at the edge of the woods,
leaving behind heart-shaped hoofprints.

By morning thin streams of water snake down the windowpanes.

A cardinal sings from the branch of a pine tree, then darts across the barnyard to peck at kitchen crumbs scattered over the melting snow.

A wagon leaves the barn, its narrow wheels cutting deeply into the snow, turning it brown. The horses' hooves grow muddy.

The sun climbs high into the blue sky. By mid-
morning a thousand tiny streams run from the
roof like a curtain of crystal beads.

Suddenly a thick sheet of snow breaks free,
slides toward the edge of the roof, and crashes
to the ground.

On a distant white hilltop a patch of brown appears. A flock of geese settles upon it, pecking at the wet grass.

Where the stream leaves the forest the ice melts away. Black
water ripples over gray stones, carving a glistening silver
line across the meadow.

All afternoon the frozen lake echoes with the snapping
and cracking of its icy surface.

On the south side of the barn the snow recedes, laying bare a small mountain of autumn hay. Three week-old lambs burrow into it and fall asleep.

By late afternoon the maple buds glow faintly red.
Buckets hanging from syrup spiles spill over into the snow.

The wagon stops along the edge of the wood. Two by two, the buckets are collected and emptied, then hung back on the trees.

Before returning to the barn the farmer pauses to watch the sun set. For the first time in months the yellow light feels warm upon his face.

"Spring," he whispers with a smile. "Spring at last."